BRENT LIBRARIES

Please return/renew this item
by the last date shown.
Books may also be renewed by
phone or online.
Tel: 0333 370 4700
On-line www.brent.gov.uk/libraryservice

by Sue Graves and Alex Paterson

Chapter 1

Mary was walking home from the bakery in Pudding Lane where she worked.

The year was **1666** and there had been no rain in London for ten months. Everywhere was hot and bone dry.

Mary looked up at the sky. She wished
it would rain but there were no clouds at all.
Mary sighed and walked on. Her feet ached
and she badly needed a drink.

Mary liked working at the bakery.

It was hard work but Mr Farriner, the baker,

was kind. Every morning, Mary helped him

light the

bread oven.

While Mr Farriner baked the bread,

Mary kept the bakery clean.

She had to sweep up the spilled flour.

She had to take the baked bread from the oven.

She had to put it to cool by the window.

She had to serve the customers, too.

Mary lived with her mother at the bottom
of Pudding Lane. Her mother looked up when
Mary came in. She was busy making a pot of soup
for their supper.

"You look hot and tired," she said. "Get a drink
of water from the pail."

Mary gulped down the water and wiped
her hand across her mouth.

"That's better," she sighed, taking some bread out
of her basket. "Mr Farriner gave us this," she said.

"That's very kind of him," said her mother.

"We'll have it with our supper."

After supper, Mary rubbed her eyes sleepily
and yawned.

"It's time you went to bed," said her mother.

"This heat is making everyone feel so tired."

Mary's bed was in the corner of the room.

It was made from a bale of straw with a blanket

on top. She climbed on to the straw and lay down.

The straw felt cool and, closing her eyes, Mary fell

fast asleep.

Chapter 2

Mary woke up with a jump. It was the middle of the night. She could smell smoke and people were shouting outside. Something was wrong. She jumped out of bed and woke her mother.

Quickly they ran outside, but the smoke was
even thicker here. Mary could hardly breathe.
People were running along the lane,
carrying leather buckets full of water.

She looked up the lane. "Look, Mother,"
she shouted. "It's the bakery. It's on fire!"
They watched as huge flames shot out of
its thatched roof.

"I must go and help Mr Farriner," said Mary.

"No, stay here," said her mother, holding on to Mary's arm. "It's too dangerous!"

But Mary wouldn't listen. Shaking off her mother's hand, she ran towards the bakery.

Mr Farriner was filling buckets with water.

"Let me help," said Mary.

Mr Farriner handed her two full buckets.

"Quick," he said. "Put out the flames in the doorway.

We've got to try and stop the fire from spreading."

Mary threw more and more water on to

the flames, but they were too strong.

The fire was getting fiercer and fiercer.

Mr Farriner and his neighbours got some large

metal hooks. They tried to pull down

the burning thatched roof. But the flames

were spreading fast from one house to the next.

Suddenly a ball of flaming thatch burst from the bakery roof.

"Look out!" yelled Mr Farriner.

The thatch crashed down. The flames spread quickly to the buildings on the opposite side of the lane. Soon they too were on fire.

People began to panic. They ran down the lane, away from the fire.

17

Mary watched with horror.

Mr Farriner grabbed her hand.

"Go back to your mother," he ordered.

"But I want to help," said Mary.

"There's nothing more we can do here,"
said Mr Farriner. "It's too dangerous for you
to stay. Run back to your mother and go down
to the river. You will be safer there."

Chapter 3

Mary ran home as fast as she could. Her cheeks were burning from the heat of the fire. She had to find her mother.

But as she got closer, she could see that her home was on fire. Mary ran to the door and hammered on it with her fists. "Mother, Mother!" she shouted, but there was no answer.

Just then Mary's neighbour, Adam, ran up.

"Come with me," he said. "You can't stay here.

It's too dangerous."

"I don't know where my mother is," said Mary,

desperately. "I've got to find her."

"Everyone is going down to the river," said Adam.

"We'll probably find her there. I have a boat.

I can row us all across safely."

Adam grabbed Mary. She struggled
but he held on tight. He pulled her along
the burning streets towards the River Thames.

The river bank was full of people. Some were

begging the ferrymen to take them across

the water. Others jumped into the river and held

on to the boats.

Adam had a small boathouse under a bridge.

Quickly he took out his boat.

"Get in, Mary," he said. "I'll row you over to the other side. You'll be safe there."

"No!" shouted Mary. She sat down on the bank and put her head in her hands. "I'm not going anywhere until I find my mother."

"Mary! Mary!"

Mary looked up. Someone was shouting her name.

She stood up and looked around. Drifts of smoke

swirled around her, making it hard to see.

Then Mary saw her mother running towards her.

"Thank goodness you're safe," she cried.

"I've been so worried," said her mother, giving Mary a big hug. "I told you to stay by me."

"I'm sorry," said Mary. "I wanted to help Mr Farriner."

Mary and her mother ran to Adam and got into
the boat as quickly as they could. Adam rowed
them out into the river. Slowly the noise
and the smoke faded into the distance.

"What will happen to us?" said Mary's mother.
She looked upset. "We have no home.
We've nothing at all."

Mary gave her mother a hug. "But we have a lot
to be thankful for," she said. "We've escaped
the fire and we're safe. We've got each other
and that's all that matters!"

Things to think about

1. What do you notice about how Mary and her mother live at the beginning of the story?
2. Why does Mary disobey her mother?
3. Do you know the real history of the Great Fire of London? How does Mary's story help you imagine it?
4. Why do you think everyone goes to the River Thames?
5. Do you think Mary is right when she says: "We have a lot to be thankful for" at the end of the story?

Write it yourself

This story is about a real event, told through the eyes of a fictional character. Now try to write your own story about a real event through the eyes of a character who was there.

Plan your story before you begin to write it.

Start off with a story map:

• a beginning to introduce the characters and where and when your story is set (the setting);

• a problem which the main characters will need to fix in the story;

• an ending where the problems are resolved.

Get writing! Try to use interesting noun phrases such as "a ball of flaming thatch" to describe your story world and excite your reader.

Notes for parents and carers

Independent reading

The aim of independent reading is to read this book with ease. This series is designed to provide an opportunity for your child to read for pleasure and enjoyment. These notes are written for you to help your child make the most of this book.

About the book

This story is about the Great Fire of London. Through the eyes of Mary, a fictional character, we see London in 1666 and witness the plight of thousands of Londoners who bravely tried to put out the flames, but then had to flee in panic, away from everything they owned.

Before reading

Ask your child why they have selected this book. Look at the title and blurb together. What do they think it will be about? Do they think they will like it?

During reading

Encourage your child to read independently. If they get stuck on a longer word, remind them that they can find syllable chunks that can be sounded out from left to right. They can also read on in the sentence and think about what would make sense.

After reading

Support comprehension by talking about the story. What happened?
Then help your child think about the messages in the book that go beyond the story, using the questions on the page opposite. Give your child a chance to respond to the story, asking:
Did you enjoy the story and why? Who was your favourite character?
What was your favourite part? What did you expect to happen at the end?

Franklin Watts
First published in Great Britain in 2018
by The Watts Publishing Group

Series Editors: Jackie Hamley and Melanie Palmer
Series Advisors: Dr Sue Bodman and Glen Franklin
Series Designer: Peter Scoulding

A CIP catalogue record for this book is
available from the British Library.

ISBN 978 1 4451 6315 4 (hbk)
ISBN 978 1 4451 6317 8 (pbk)
ISBN 978 1 4451 6316 1 (library ebook)

Printed in China

Franklin Watts
An imprint of
Hachette Children's Group
Part of The Watts Publishing Group
Carmelite House
50 Victoria Embankment
London EC4Y 0DZ

An Hachette UK Company
www.hachette.co.uk

www.franklinwatts.co.uk